Lily and the Gift Planet Earth

MW00930928

Lily and the Gift Planet Earth
Copyright © 2021 by Colette B Ramazani

All rights reserved. No part of this publication may be reproduced, distributed,
or transmitted in any form or by any means, including photocopying, recording, or other
electronic or mechanical methods, without the prior written permission of the author,
except in the case of brief quotations embodied in critical reviews and certain
other non-commercial uses permitted by copyright law.

This also includes conveying via e-mail without permission in writing from the author.
This book is for entertainment purposes only. All work is fiction creation from the mind of the author,
all persons or places relating to real-life characters or locations are purely coincidental.

Tellwell Talent
www.tellwell.ca

ISBN
978-0-2288-5060-1 (Hardcover)
978-0-2288-5061-8 (Paperback)

Lily and the Gift Planet Earth

Written by Colette B Ramazani

Introduction

Did you know that everything ever made comes from one place? It sounds impossible, right? So where is this mystical land from which everything is born?

The answer is Planet Earth!

Not only does Earth provide us with our food, water, and homes, but it also provides the resources that we turn into our clothes, computers, jewelry, shoes – and that's just to name a few things!

Planet Earth really is a gift, and it's a gift we shouldn't take for granted. It is the first thing all children see when leaving their mother's tummies, and the last thing the elderly see before departing. It truly is a gift from God, the Creator of all that is and ever will be!

Planet Earth provides for all of our needs! But did you know that we don't look after it the way we should?

What will our future be if we don't protect Planet Earth? What will happen to our brothers and sisters, our sons and daughters, and the generations to come?

The gift of Planet Earth is your gift, too. It's your gift to enjoy and your gift to pass on to the next generation. Each one of us can help preserve Planet Earth. If we treat it right, we can then pass that same magnificent gift on to our children. But we can only do this if we conserve and preserve Planet Earth with the love and care it deserves.

After all, Planet Earth has looked after humans for hundreds of thousands of years! Now it's our turn to pay Mother Earth back.

The Earth - My Gift

Earth is a place of life.

"I admire Planet Earth's extraordinary beauty! There are so many things given to us by Planet Earth," says Lily

"Lily, are you ready to go to the park?" asks Mom.

"I keep looking at the new globe that Nana and Poppa gave me. It's so strange to think that everything that has ever happened has happened on this blue and green globe."

"Truly, Grandpa and Grandma passed this wonderful globe to you, hoping you would learn to appreciate and protect our Planet Earth. One generation to the next," says Mom, winking at Lily.

"I understand, Mom, and I will always protect my globe! I am the future of my planet. I'm so happy to call Planet Earth my home."

"Let's go," says Mom, looking at the clock. "Your father is waiting and we're meeting your friend Emma and her parents."

"Yippee, parks are awesome!" says Lily. "They have so much greenery and space and they're such peaceful places to play!"

"Oh!" Lily says with a grin when they get to the park. "There's Emma and her dog, Max."

Mischievously, Lily quickly hides behind a tree, holding her globe.

"Lily, where are you?" shouts Emma.

"Arf! Arf!" says Max.

"Look what I've got, Emma! I want to tell you all about the thing I cherish most."

"What is that?" says Emma, with a strange look on her face.

"It's a special gift from my grandparents!"

"Oh wonderful, Lily! Is that your grandparents' globe?"

"Yes. It's called Planet Earth. It's where you and I and everyone lives, even your cute dog, Max. It's where all of history has happened, and where the future is yet to happen. I really love it unconditionally."

"But what does unconditionally mean?"

"My Mom told me," says Lily, "that to love something unconditionally means to love it no matter what, and I do!"

"I guess I have a lot of things to learn!"

"Emma, shall we go on an adventure?"

"Definitely!"

As the girls walk through the forest at the back of the park, Lily says,

"Emma, Planet Earth is a gift for every single one of us. It needs to be *protected*."

"How can we help protect our Planet Earth from anything harmful?"

"Simple, Emma! We should not hunt animals for sport. We should not chop down trees. We should not litter or start fires in places like this fascinating forest."

"Some people do that?" asks Emma, horrified.

"Oh, yes," says Lily. "Previous generations did their best to conserve and preserve the land and forests so that we can still enjoy them today. Nowadays, though, entire forests are disappearing because of greediness!"

Emma shakes her head in disbelief. "I didn't know that!"

"These trees aren't just places for the birds to live. Trees and plants give us the air we breathe," says Lily.

"Just imagine if previous generations hadn't cared to protect our Planet Earth. We wouldn't have any trees or fresh air. We would be in big trouble."

"I agree, Lily."

"Marvelous trees, birds, deer and bunnies live in the forest," says Lily. "It's home to so many things. Forest fires can affect all life in the forest. Luckily, airplanes can drop fire retardants to help control the fires and firefighters can work on the ground to put the fires out. People do their best to help Planet Earth."

"Wow! Well, if our parents and grandparents looked after Planet Earth for us, then we need to make sure that we look after it, too," says Emma.

"Planet Earth needs our help, for sure," says Emma.

"The *oceans are rising* and the *temperatures are changing* too. This is climate change and global warming. We must be aware of the dangers of our actions that affect the *Earth's atmosphere*," says Lily.

"Come on Emma."

"Great, I'm very excited to see where we're going next."

"Can you guess what our next adventure will be?" asks Lily.

Golden Gate Bridge, San Francisco, California
Fire threaten the region, Summer 2020

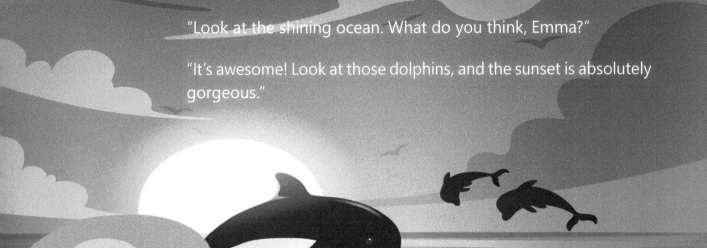

"Look at the shining ocean. What do you think, Emma?"

"It's awesome! Look at those dolphins, and the sunset is absolutely gorgeous."

"There is nothing more beautiful than Planet Earth. Maybe my mom, but I am allowed to say that!" says Lily.

"My mom, too!" laughs Emma. "But seriously, I think I'm beginning to understand why you love Planet Earth. I love it too."

"Wonderful, Emma! What's not to love on our planet?"

As the girls hop into a small rowboat, Lily says,

"Being on the water is so much fun. A whole other world is going on just beneath us as we paddle."

"But people don't think of the ocean like that, do they, Lily?"

"They don't take good care to protect the ocean because they can't see the sea life themselves," explains Lily. "I'll never forget about all the wonders underwater that we know are there. *Truly, the ocean, is a precious gift to us,*" she says.

"I can't imagine life without our oceans," says Lily.

"There will be no life if they disappear," exclaims Emma.

"When I come here with my parents, I love to just stare out at the ocean and watch the awesome waves as they roll after each other before crashing onto the beach." says Lily

Emma smiles, "Well, I usually just put on my swimsuit and jump straight in! The waves are amazing though, aren't they? Even Max is happy to see the waves."

"Yes, Emma! They are incredible," replies Lily.

"The beach is one of my favorite places to visit," says Lily.

"What child doesn't like a sandy shore?" replies Emma.

"It's amazing that nature powers the wind and the wind powers the waves, and they just do what they do...forever!"

"I hope the oceans will live forever, Lily!"

"I think with our help, Emma, they will! The biggest problem is the trash thrown into the oceans. The plastic and rubbish that get dumped are hurting, trapping, and killing the ocean life."

"That's terrible!" says Emma. "I didn't know any of this."

"Most of the trash is underneath the ocean's surface, so it's hard to see. And do you want to know something really bad?" asks Lily, with a very serious look on her face.

"I'm not sure I do," replies Emma.

"There's a river just on the other side of the park called 'Tiger River.' You will be shocked to see how people have treated it."

"Here it is. What do you see, Emma?"

"TRASH! I'm shocked! My heart is broken."

"I know, Emma! You and I are the future. We need to get all of our rivers and oceans clean."

"Just you and me? That will take an awfully long time!"

"Not just you and I alone, but our generation," says Lily. "If everyone can find it within themselves to care, we can fix these problems."

"The trash is mostly plastic bottles and plastic packaging floating on the water. Why can't people use the trash cans?" asks Emma.

"People could throw their plastic rubbish into the trash, but recycling is much better!" says Lily. "It means the plastic gets used again!"

"Recycling. Yes, that is exactly right. I agree that our generation can be the one to change the course of Planet Earth," says Emma.

"I think we should talk to our parents about this. They may be able to help us start an environmental organization in the community to address this problem." says Lily

"Guess what, Emma? I have an idea for our next look at nature."

"Oh, what is it?"

"It's a surprise, but it's definitely something that will cheer us up," replies Lily.

"It's a valley, Emma! Isn't it divine?

"It's stunning beyond words! It's bursting with different colors!"

"It absolutely has *one-of-a-kind* beauty," adds Lily. "Flower - filled mountain valleys are the best."

"I love the different shades of color and the sheer wonders of the valley!" exclaims Emma.

"When my parents and I go to the park, I always ask to come here to see the amazing mountains and valley. It's awe-inspiring."

The girls fixed their attention on the valley, with big beaming smiles on their faces.

"Emma, our precious Planet Earth is our home."

"There's so much to see and explore, Lily! We're so lucky, but some people just don't seem to realize it!"

"I agree. I'm glad I got to share this gift of Planet Earth with you and talk about ways we can help it. Look around us! Everything feels so good! Even the birds and butterflies are enjoying themselves. Max is enjoying himself too!"

"Arf! Arf!"

"Thank you, Planet Earth, for being a blessing to all of us. It is time for us to fight for you," says Lily.

"Surely, Planet Earth must live forever," declares Emma.

"We are the future of our planet," says Lily.

"Lily, adventuring with you has been fun. Nature is beautiful and precious."

"It sure is, Emma. I can't wait for our next adventure together! I overheard our parents talking about an African safari vacation!"

Acknowledgements

I have so many wonderful people to thank for helping me on my writing journey!

To my Mama Regine and Baba Kabese, who brought me into this world.

To my brother, Pierre, and my sisters Albertine, Zaina, Leontine, and Monique, who raised me and sacrificed a lot to send me to school at an early age. They led me in just the right direction I needed to get a higher education.

To Marceline, my sister and best friend, whose love helped fuel me on my journey.

A huge thank you to Josephine, and all of my nieces and nephews, who have loved me unconditionally and looked up to me as their role model.

To my health care team who never gave up on me. Without them, I would not have been able to create this adventure.

Thank you so much to Jodie and her entire family for making me feel like part of their family!

A special thanks to my best friend, Shane, and her entire family who loved me unconditionally from the first day we met at church.

I owe a huge debt of gratitude to Dr. Joseph E. Mwantuali (including his family) for allowing me the opportunity to give a voice to the voiceless through our book: Tell This to My Mother.

To Rena, her husband Keris (founder of CongoSwim), and the entire team from LOPC (Lafayette – Orinda Presbyterian Church) in Lafayette, California. They wrapped me in their arms with love. They gave me the strength to carry on another day.

To my special angel, sent to watch over me since my arrival in this part of the world.

Thank you so much to all of you from the bottom of my heart! I believe that my mother is looking down from heaven right now, happy to see that there are still compassionate human beings in the world – people who have looked after me and lifted me up to become who I am today. I'M FOREVER GRATEFUL!

Author's Note

Most parents who take time to observe their children will notice certain inherent traits. These traits develop throughout childhood and continue into adulthood. Just like Lily, I have been fascinated by the beauty of this planet that we live on, called Earth.

Early in my life, I wanted to learn more about where water comes from, how trees grow, and why some of them are small and others tall. I wondered why flowers grow in different colors, and what life would be like if we didn't have this wonderful nature. If we destroy these things, what will happen? ALL of nature is significant! Each thing plays a role for us, and we for them.

I have been attached to many elements that form the Earth in different ways. I care for these elements (nature) so much.

I have valued them since I was a little girl, not only for the beauty they represent but also for what they give us, such as clean air, water, food, shelter, trees, and medicine, etc. Without these elements, there is no life – no animals, birds, fish, insects . . . or humans! Including me!

Since Lily and I love and have concern for this Planet Earth, as portrayed in this book, our desire is for all people to notice and appreciate, even more, this magnificent, fascinating creation! And we wish this precious Earth will continue to be enjoyed, generation after generation.

I believe that people, more and more, will come to see the same dangers of global warming that Lily and I see. Dangers that threaten our planet. We have a responsibility to save our only HOME!

The fear Lily and I have is climate change. If we don't act now and protect our beloved Planet Earth, it could lead to the destruction of all humans.

Lily is a little girl, who may have a different name from me, but just like me, Lily sees the unique beauty in everything in front of her. We both admire the beauty that Planet Earth holds. The well-being of Planet Earth is important to the existence of humans, and therefore, we should treat this gift as if our existence depends on it forever. Because it does! This is a fact, that we all need to face.

Lily and I believe it is going to take collective work from every living human being to save it.

CPSIA information can be obtained
at www.ICGtesting.com
Printed in the USA
BVHW091202310821
615693BV00018B/1107